# My Friends the Frogs

stories and pictures by James Marshall

Donna Alvermann
Connie A. Bridge
Barbara A. Schmidt
Lyndon W. Searfoss
Peter Winograd

 **D.C. Heath and Company**
Lexington, Massachusetts   Toronto, Ontario

# Acknowledgments

Grateful acknowledgment is made for permission to reprint the following copyrighted material.

Silverstein, Shel. "**The Lost Cat**," from *A Light in the Attic: Poems and Drawings of Shel Silverstein*. Copyright © 1981 by Snake Eye Music, Inc. Reprinted by permission of Harper & Row, Publishers, Inc.

***Cover and Illustrations***  James Marshall.
***Cover Design***  Studio Goodwin-Sturges.

***Editorial***  Book Editor:  Susan D. Paro. **Editorial Services:**  Marianna Frew Palmer, K. Kirschbaum Harvie. **Permissions Editor:**  Dorothy B. McLeod.

***Series Design***  Leslie Dews.  ***Book Design***  Jennifer Levey, Ingrid Cooper.  ***Production***  Mary Hunter. ***Photo Coordinator***  Connie Komack.  ***Photo Research***  Nina Whitney.  ***Photo Styling***  June Martin.

***Photography***  Ken O'Donoghue © D.C. Heath.

# Table of Contents

# The New Hat

A rat made a new hat.

"I like my hat," she said.
"Now I will go out."

"Hello. Do you like my new hat?"
said the rat.

"Yes, but put this on it,"
said the dog.

"Hello. Do you like my new hat?"
said the rat.

"Yes, but put this on it,"
said the bird.

"Hello. Do you like my new hat?"
said the rat.

"Yes, but put this on it,"
said the cat.

"Hello. Do you like my new hat?"
said the rat.

"Yes, but put this on it,"
said the fish.

"Hello. Do you like my new hat?"
said the rat.

The horse ate the hat.

"Yes, I do like your hat!"
said the horse.

"Will you dance with me?"
said the cow.

"No," said the pig.
"You will step on my toes."

"Will you dance with me?"
said the cow.

"No," said the cat.
"You will step on my tail."

"Will you dance with me?"
said the cow.

"No," said the dog.
"You will step on my ears."

"Who will dance with me?"
said the cow.

"I will, I will!"
said the bird.

"You will?" said the cow.

"Yes, I will," said the bird.

"I am ready to dance!"
said the cow.

"Look at them go!"
said the pig.

# I See You

"I see you!" said the bird.
"I see you, rabbit!"

"Go home," said the rabbit.
"I have to sleep."

"I see you!" said the bird.
"I see you, duck!"

"Go home," said the duck.
"I have to read."

"This bird may not stay,"
said the rabbit.

"No," said the duck.

"I see you!" said the bird.
"I see you, fox!"

"Go home," said the fox.
"I have to eat."

"A fox!" said the rabbit.

"Run!" said the duck.

The rabbit and the duck ran home.
This made the fox mad.

The fox ran home.

"Do I have to go home?"
said the bird.

"No," said the rabbit and the duck.
"We need you!"

# The Fine Hat

"What a fine hat,"
said the yellow dog.

"Thank you," said the brown dog.
"It is new."

"I am sad," said the yellow dog.
"I want a new hat too."

"Hello," said the red hen.
"Do you like my new hat?"

"It is a fine hat,"
said the yellow dog.

"Thank you," said the red hen.

"Now I am **very** sad,"
said the yellow dog.
"I want a new hat too!"

"Hello," said the white cat.
"Do you like my new hat?"

"It is a fine hat,"
said the yellow dog.

"Thank you," said the white cat.

"Now I am mad!"
said the yellow dog.
"I want a new hat!"

"Put us back!"
said the blue bird.
"Put us back!"

"My, my," said the yellow dog.

"What a fine hat,"
said the brown dog.

"Thank you," said the yellow dog.
"It is new."

# Let's Make a Hat

Let's make a hat!
This is how you do it.

1. Cut some paper that will go on your head. Tape it like this.

2. Cut some paper that is
   like this.

3. Now tape the paper on the hat
   like this.

Put your hat on your head.
How do you look?
Is your hat a fine hat?

## THE LOST CAT

We can't find the cat,
We don't know where she's at,
Oh, where did she go?
Does anyone know?
Let's ask this walking hat.

—Shel Silverstein
from A LIGHT IN THE ATTIC

# The Funny Fox

"I am a funny fox,"
said the fox.
"Now I will do some
very funny things."

"Look out! Here I come!"
said the fox.

"Help!" said the cat.

"That is not funny!"
said the cat.

"I think it is very funny,"
said the fox.

"Look out! Here I come!"
said the fox.

"Help!" said the dog.

"That is not funny!"
said the dog.

"I think it is very funny,"
said the fox.

"Look out! Here I come!"
said the fox.

"Help!" said Mom.

"I made that cake for you,"
said Mom.

"That is not funny!"
said the fox.
"That is not funny at all!"

"Here comes Pig,"
said Rabbit.

"Oh no! Look at Pig!"
said Frog.

"Hello, Pig," said Rabbit.

"Good to see you, Pig,"
said Frog.

"Rats," said Pig.

"How did you know who I was?"

"We just did," said Frog.

"Look!" said Rabbit.
"Here comes Pig."

"Hello, Pig," said Frog.
"Good to see you."

"How did you know who I was?"
said Pig.

"We just did," said Frog.
"We just did."

"Look!" said Rabbit.
"Who is that?"

"It is not Pig,"
said Frog.

"No," said Rabbit.
"Pig is not that tall."

"Who is it?"
said Frog.

"Pig!" said Pig.

"Oh my!" said Frog.
"We did not know it was you!"

"Good for Pig!" said Rabbit.
"Good for Pig!"

"I want a pet," said Mr. Dog.

"I do too," said Mrs. Dog.
"Let's go to the pet shop."

"We want a pet," said Mr. Dog.

"Here is a yellow bird,"
said the man.

"What a fine bird," said Mrs. Dog.
"It will be a good pet."

"Oh good," said the yellow bird.
"May I bring my friend the cat?"

"Yes, you may," said Mr. Dog.

"Oh good," said the cat.
"May I bring my friend the pig?"

"Yes, you may," said Mrs. Dog.

"Oh good," said the pig.
"May I bring my friends the frogs?"

"Yes, you may," said Mr. Dog.

"Now we will go home,"
said Mrs. Dog.

"May I go with you?" said the man.
"You have all my pets!"

"Yes," said Mr. and Mrs. Dog.
"Let's all go home."

# The Gingerbread Man